Princess ANGELICA

Junior Reporter

Princess ANGELICA

Junior Reporter

Monique Polak

Illustrated by **Jane Heinrichs**

ORCA BOOK PUBLISHERS

Library and Archives Canada Cataloguing in Publication
Title: Princess Angelica, junior reporter / Monique Polak ; illustrated by Jane Heinrichs.
Names: Polak, Monique, author. | Heinrichs, Jane, 1982– illustrator.
Series: Orca echoes.
Description: Series statement: Orca echoes
Identifiers: Canadiana (print) 20190169060 | Canadiana (ebook) 20190169079 |
ISBN 9781459823587 (softcover) | ISBN 9781459823594 (PDF) | ISBN 9781459823600 (EPUB)
Classification: LCC PS8631.O43 P75 2020 | DDC jC813/.6—dc23

Library of Congress Control Number: 2019943995
Simultaneously published in Canada and the United States in 2020

Summary: In this illustrated early chapter book, Angelica is
mistaken for a junior reporter at her local newspaper.

*Orca Book Publishers is committed to reducing the consumption of nonrenewable resources in the
making of our books. We make every effort to use materials that support a sustainable future.*

Orca Book Publishers gratefully acknowledges the support for its publishing
programs provided by the following agencies: the Government of Canada,
the Canada Council for the Arts and the Province of British Columbia
through the BC Arts Council and the Book Publishing Tax Credit.

Cover artwork and interior illustrations by Jane Heinrichs
Author photo by John Fredericks

ORCA BOOK PUBLISHERS
orcabook.com

Printed and bound in Canada.

23 22 21 20 • 4 3 2 1

Chapter One

We're supposed to be going to the park for a swim.

Joon and I have sunscreen, towels and water in reusable bottles. I also have coconut oil because they were giving away samples at the corner store. The man who gave me the packet said coconut oil can be used for many purposes, including cooking and applying to scraped knees and elbows to speed up healing.

Joon and I spot the balloons at the same time. They are hard to miss—there are several clusters of them in front of the building across from the park.

"It's opening day at the new library," I tell Joon. "They must be having a party. Let's check it out."

"What about our swim?" Joon asks.

"We can swim later."

"Do you think there will be cake?" Joon asks.

"I don't know. Eating isn't usually allowed in libraries. They don't want people leaving crumbs on the books."

"Maybe there'll be cake *outside* the library," Joon says as we cross the street.

There is a crowd by the entrance. A band is playing music, and there is a table with lemonade and a stack of brochures.

Ms. MacLean, the head librarian, is pouring lemonade into paper cups. She has curly purple hair and turquoise eyeglasses. "Welcome, Jelly and Joon!" Ms. MacLean says, putting down the lemonade jug so she can shake our hands. "Be sure to take one of these brochures about our programs and our hours of business."

Ms. MacLean knows us from the old library, which was just two rooms in an old house.

"Congratulations on your new library!" Joon says to Ms. MacLean. "This one will have room for a lot more books. I hope you're getting a raise!"

Ms. MacLean laughs. "Have a look inside, girls. You are right—there is a lot more room for books! There is also room for many other exciting things. But first I have something special for you two!"

"Is it edible?" Joon asks.

"Not unless you eat paper and drink ink!" Ms. MacLean takes her briefcase from under the table, reaches in and gives us each a spiral notebook. She also gives us each a pen that says *Readers Rule*.

This library is huge. It has three floors and giant glass windows. In the middle is an atrium, a large open area with a glass ceiling. There are desks for reading and studying, like in the old library. But this library also has couches, armchairs and even beanbags for sitting on.

The staircase is wide enough for twenty people to sit on every step. When we reach the top, Joon and I turn to look back at the ground floor. "Those stairs are like benches in an auditorium. The library could put on shows here. Like when that author came to talk at the old library last year."

"It must have cost a lot of money to build this place," Joon says. "My dad says spending money to build libraries is a waste. He says nobody goes to the library anymore. He says people can find all the information they need online."

"Look over there," I tell Joon. I point to several bookcases filled with DVDs. There are cartoons, adventure movies, documentaries and more. "And look over there," I say, lifting my chin to a door with a sign that says *Multimedia* and then to a sign with the letter *B* and two down arrows and the words *Rare Books*. That must be in the basement.

A rare-books room would be a good place to hang out on a rainy day.

"Your dad might be wrong about nobody going to the library anymore," I tell Joon. "There's tons to do at this library. I don't know about you, but something tells me we'll be coming here a lot."

We take a smaller staircase to the third floor, where there are offices and study rooms. There is also another large open area with sofas and bookshelves. This is called the Newspaper and Magazine Department.

Joon nudges my elbow. "My dad says nobody reads paper newspapers anymore. He says everyone gets their news online."

Someone is sitting on a couch, reading the *Montreal Gazette*. Because the newspaper is spread out in front of the person's face, I can't see who it is.

"I prefer a paper newspaper," a voice says from behind the newspaper.

When the person peeks her head out, I recognize Eloise, a girl from our school.

"What are you doing here, Eloise?" Joon asks.

"What does it look like I'm doing? I'm reading the newspaper! Not everyone gets their news online," Eloise says.

"What are you reading about?" Joon asks her.

Eloise puts the newspaper down. "I'm reading an article about how people get ideas. I just read about a painter who gets his ideas in the shower!"

"Speaking of showers," Joon says, "is there a bathroom close by?"

Eloise says there is a bathroom near the offices.

"I'll be right back," Joon tells me.

"Who wrote that article you're reading?" I ask Eloise.

Eloise picks up the newspaper. "The reporter's name is…Angelica Ledoux." Eloise's eyes dart from the newspaper to me, then to the spiral notebook and pen in my hands. "Angelica! That's your name too, right? Maybe you wrote this story!" Eloise says with a laugh.

I could say no.

After all, I made myself a promise that I would stop making up stories. I got myself into a jam when I told the girls at summer camp I was a princess. Then there was the time at the animal-rescue center when I told my friends I was a lion trainer.

But this is an irresistible opportunity.

"I did write it!" I tell Eloise. I click on my pen. "I'm Angelica Ledoux, junior reporter."

Chapter Two

You'd think nothing would go wrong in a newly built library, but it turns out there's a problem with the book-return drop.

People are supposed to use the slot to return books when the library is closed. I don't even know why someone would bother testing it out today, when the library is open and there's a band playing outside. But someone decides to test the drop, and when they do, it makes such a loud *screech* we can hear it on the third floor.

It's so loud that even the band stops playing.

Eloise and I rush to the window. We see a boy outside covering his ears. Then we hear the loud squeal again.

Eloise shakes her head. "Nobody will be able to get any reading done in this library with a racket like that."

Joon returns from the bathroom. "What was that horrible noise?" she asks. "I could hear it even when the water was running."

Eloise explains that the screech seems to be coming from the book-drop slot. "I hope Ms. MacLean can find someone to fix it."

"I bet Jelly can fix it," Joon tells Eloise. "Jelly is good at fixing things. She's also good at making up—"

"Let's go downstairs and look at that slot," I say, interrupting Joon before she can tell Eloise about my talent for inventing stories. I don't want Joon to tell Eloise how I fooled the girls at summer camp into believing I was a princess or how I once pretended to be a lion trainer.

"Do you carry around a repair kit?" Eloise asks me.

"Jelly doesn't need a repair kit. Her repairs start here." Joon taps the side of her head.

The three of us race down the stairs. When we get outside, we find Ms. MacLean examining the book drop's mechanism. The bandleader is with her. When Ms. MacLean opens and closes the slot, it makes the loud screech. The bandleader covers his ears.

"I don't understand how a brand-new book drop can make such a terrible noise. I'm afraid we'll have to wait till Monday for the custodian to fix it," says Ms. MacLean. When she sees Joon and me, she calls out, "Could you girls ask one of the assistant librarians to make a sign that says *Broken Book Drop. Do Not Use*?"

"We *could* ask one of the assistant librarians to do that," Joon says. "But maybe you should let Jelly have a look first. She's very good at repairing things."

The bandleader raises his eyebrows. "A child who's good at repairing things?"

"Children can do repairs. And children can lead bands," I tell him. "Children can't drive cars, but they can do a lot of other things. Now if you don't mind, could you move over so I can have a look at that slot?"

The bandleader moves over.

A crowd is gathered near the entrance. "This could be a little noisy," I warn them. Then I turn to the bandleader. "Maybe you and your band could play an extra-loud song."

"Certainly," the bandleader says.

People sing, clap and stomp their feet as the band plays "When the Saints Go Marching In."

They hardly notice the screeching sound when I open the slot.

"What do you think is wrong with it?" Joon asks me.

"I don't know yet," I say without looking up. I open and close the slot again. Then I turn to Ms. MacLean. "The problem seems to be coming from the right hinge. A little oil should do the trick."

"Oil?" Ms. MacLean says. "I suppose I could send one of the assistant librarians to the hardware store for some oil. Do we need a particular kind?"

I raise one finger in the air. I do that when I get a good idea. "Joon, do you mind passing me a packet of coconut oil?"

I apply a few dabs of oil to the slot's right hinge. When I'm done, I wipe away the excess.

"Do you really think that will fix the problem?" Eloise asks.

"There's only one way to find out." I step away from the book drop. "Ms. MacLean, would you like to try it?"

As Ms. MacLean is about to open the slot, the boy we saw earlier covers his ears again. Even the bandleader looks worried.

There is no screech when Ms. MacLean opens the slot.

There is no screech when she closes it.

"Nice job, Jelly!" Ms. MacLean says, shaking my hand for the second time that day.

There is a flash of light and the click of a camera. Someone snaps my photograph.

"And who are you?" Ms. MacLean asks the photographer.

"My name is Hubert St-Onge. I work for the *Gazette*," he says.

I pose for a photo, smiling as I hold up the empty coconut-oil packet.

Eloise is watching. "You must know Jelly from your office," she says to Monsieur St-Onge.

The photographer shrugs. "No. I don't think we've ever met."

I don't have much time to come up with an answer. Luckily, like all reporters, I can handle tight deadlines. "I'm a freelance reporter," I say to Eloise and Monsieur St-Onge. "I write my stories at home and submit them by email. That way I never have to go to the office."

"Good to meet you, Jelly," Monsieur St-Onge says. "Nice work on the book-return slot!"

Chapter Three

Being in the air-conditioned library was nice, but now it's time for that swim in the park pool.

Joon and I are splashing each other in the shallow end. The lifeguard blows her whistle when a boy gets too close to the lanes reserved for adults doing laps.

Because there are so many swimmers, three adults have to share two lanes.

One swimmer does the butterfly, lifting her shoulders out of the water with every stroke. The other two are doing the breaststroke. One wears a bathing cap with plastic flowers.

Even over the sounds of children laughing, Joon and I can make out angry voices coming from the lap lanes.

"It sounds like a fight," Joon whispers.

The three adults have stopped swimming. Two are waving their arms and shouting.

I tug on Joon's wrist. "Let's swim over and see what's going on!"

Joon shakes her head. "We shouldn't do that, Jelly. It isn't any of our business."

I straighten my shoulders and puff up my chest. "It may not be any of *your* business, Joon, but it's *my* business. I've decided to become a junior reporter."

"A junior reporter?" Joon asks. "Jelly, are you making up stories again?"

"I'm not *making up* stories," I tell her. "I'm *investigating* them. You may not know this, Joon, but reporters have to be able to *sniff out* stories." I tap the tip of Joon's nose. "And I smell a story at the other side of the pool!"

Joon taps the tip of her own nose. "You know what I smell, Jelly? I smell trouble. And we should *stay out of trouble*!"

"Trouble is exactly what makes a story interesting!" I say. "And trouble sells newspapers! No one wants to read a story about how well swimmers get along in the lap lanes. Everyone wants to read about trouble there! That could be my approach. 'Trouble in the Lap Lane, by Angelica Ledoux.'"

"Who's Angelica Ledoux?" Joon asks. "Your last name is Elmslie."

"Right," I say. "Of course it is. I don't know why I said Ledoux. Are you or aren't you coming with me to investigate?"

"Okay, I'm coming," Joon says.

We swim to the other end of the pool. The lifeguard is trying to settle the swimmers' argument.

A man wags his finger in the air. "You splashed me while you were doing the butterfly!" he says.

"If you come to a pool, you should expect to get splashed!" the other swimmer answers.

"You're not allowed to do the butterfly during lap swim," the third swimmer says. She turns to the lifeguard. "Isn't that true?"

The lifeguard looks from the woman who was doing the butterfly to the man who complained and then to the woman who said the butterfly is not allowed during lap swim. "Actually, that isn't on the list of rules," she says, and the three swimmers start to shout at each other all over again.

"You see!" says the woman who was doing the butterfly.

"It *should* be a rule!" the other woman says.

I swim closer to the lanes where the adults are arguing. "Excuse me," I say, "but if you don't mind, I'd like to ask a few questions."

"This is none of your business," the butterfly swimmer says. "Besides, you're just a child."

"I may be a child," I tell her, "but I am also a reporter. I'm working on a story about the fights people get into at the pool." I turn to the lifeguard. "Does this happen a lot?" I ask.

"You wouldn't believe the fights people get into," she says. " 'You're swimming so slow you're holding up traffic!' 'Quit bumping into me, bozo!' " The lifeguard chuckles.

"Did you just call me bozo?" the butterfly swimmer asks her.

"No, no. Not at all," the lifeguard stammers.

I grab the edge of the pool and pull myself up onto the deck. "I'm going to get my pen and notepad. I'd like to take some notes for my story. And oh, I nearly forgot to introduce myself. I'm Angelica Ledoux, junior reporter."

Chapter Four

It's a good thing we did a unit in English class on writing for a newspaper.

Miss Marston taught us how to do an interview and organize our notes. For the final assignment, we had to write a newspaper story based on our research. Miss Marston gave us a deadline. We had exactly sixty minutes. Because she wanted us to experience what being a newspaper reporter feels like, Miss Marston walked around the classroom, telling us to hurry up.

At first the woman who was doing the butterfly doesn't want to talk to me, but when she hears the other two swimmers telling their sides of the story, she changes her mind. In no time I have four pages of notes.

I write down every word they tell me. I also remember something else Miss Marston taught us—the details make a newspaper story come alive. So I jot down some notes about the flowery bathing cap and how the woman who did the butterfly has muscular shoulders.

The lifeguard says I can interview her later, during her break.

When I've asked all the questions I can think of and recorded as many interesting details as possible, Joon and I leave the pool area and go to relax under a tree. We spread our towels out side by side.

"When will your story appear in the paper?" Joon asks. "Do you think it will make the front page?"

"Uh, I only just started the research," I answer. "I still need to interview the lifeguard. I also need to find more examples of trouble in the lap lanes."

"That shouldn't be a problem," Joon says.

After that Joon and I stare up at the clouds. "See that one?" she asks, pointing to a cloud directly overhead. "Doesn't it look like a house? See the roof?"

"What about that one?" I say. "It looks like a lawn mower."

We are still looking at clouds when someone spreads out a towel next to us. It's Eloise. There is a woman with her who must be her mother.

Eloise introduces us. "This is Jelly, which is short for Angelica Le—"

"Nice to meet you," I interrupt, sitting up and reaching out to shake Eloise's mother's hand. "This is Joon."

"Pleased to meet you," Eloise's mother says to us.

"Jelly is the girl I told you about. She used coconut oil to fix the book-return slot at the library," Eloise tells her mother.

"She's also a reporter," Joon adds. "Jelly is working on a story for the *Gazette*."

Eloise's mother removes her sunglasses so she can take a better look at me. "Aren't you a little young to work for a newspaper?"

"I'm a junior reporter," I say, hoping this is enough of an explanation to end this part of the conversation. "The *Gazette* is trying to find ways to get more kids to read the newspaper. They want to build a younger readership."

"That sounds like a good idea," Eloise's mother says.

Her reaction gives me the incredible feeling I get when someone believes one of my made-up stories!

It's time for Joon to go home for her Korean lesson, and Eloise's mom wants to have a quick swim before she goes back to her office. So Eloise and I are left lying under the tree.

Eloise is curious about my career as a reporter. "Who's the most famous person you've interviewed?" she asks.

"The prime minister of Canada." He's the first person who comes to my mind.

"Was he nice?"

"Super nice. He said that of the thousands of people who had interviewed him, I was his favorite."

"You were?" Eloise is impressed. "Did someone take a photo of the two of you together?"

For a second I am stumped. But then an answer comes to me. "The story I wrote was about the prime minister, not me. It wouldn't have been right for me to be in the photograph."

"What was your angle?" Eloise asks.

Eloise asks tough questions. Maybe she should consider becoming a reporter too! "We focused on the future. I asked him what kind of world today's children can expect to inherit."

"What was his answer?"

"He said something I will never forget."

Eloise sits up on her elbows. "What was it?"

"He said, 'When today's children grow up, they will need to repair some of the damage that's been done to our planet. But by using their brains to solve problems, and by always being honest, I believe they will make this a better world.'"

"Wow!" says Eloise. "How inspiring!"

I'm inspired too. I definitely want to use my knack for repairing things to improve our planet.

I also feel a little guilty. Making up a story about being a reporter and interviewing the prime minister isn't exactly honest.

Chapter Five

Feeling guilty is not fun. I am going to lie under this tree and think about my story instead. I will focus my research on trouble in the lap lanes.

Miss Marston said newspaper stories need focus.

When I interviewed the lifeguard before, she told me she sees arguments in the lap lanes almost every day, especially when many swimmers share the lanes.

Mostly, she said, people argue about others swimming too slowly and holding up everyone else.

But it turns out there are other kinds of trouble in the lanes. I discover this when I hear a woman shouting, "Help me! Please!"

It's Eloise's mother. At first I think maybe she got a cramp, but that isn't it at all.

She's lost an earring.

"I know I was wearing two earrings when I went into the pool," she tells the lifeguard who is now on duty. This lifeguard is a boy. "I touched my ears and felt them. Please help me find that earring! It belonged to my grandmother."

"I'll do my best," the lifeguard promises. "Can you show me the other

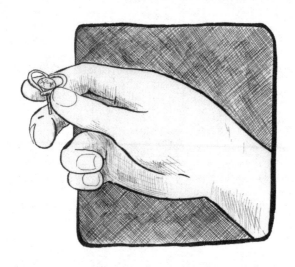

earring so I know what we're looking for?"

Eloise's mother unclips the earring from her ear. It is a small gold earring with a green stone.

The lifeguard examines it. "It won't be easy to find such a small earring."

Eloise's mother gets a wild look in her eyes. "But you said you'd do your best!"

The lifeguard finds a colleague and asks her to watch the pool. Then he goes to the equipment shack for a snorkel and mask. "I'll scour the bottom of the pool," he tells Eloise's mother.

It takes a long time for him to check the pool, which can't be a good sign. If he'd found the earring, he'd be back by now.

Eloise's mother wrings her hands.

"At least you have the other earring," Eloise tells her.

That does not cheer her up. "What good is one earring?" she asks.

"You could make it into a ring," I suggest.

Eloise's mother ignores my suggestion. The lifeguard comes up to the surface, but only for some air. He pops right down again. He does this several more times before he finally gets out of the pool. It's obvious from his hunched shoulders that he has not found the earring. "Sorry," he tells Eloise's mother, "no luck."

"Can you drain the pool?" Eloise's mother asks.

"Uh," the lifeguard says, "I don't think that's a good idea. Not during the hottest week of the summer so far. It would take an entire day to drain the pool and another day to fill it back up. People wouldn't be very happy about that."

"But what about my earring?" Eloise's mother looks as if she is about to cry.

"I have an idea!" I say.

This time Eloise's mother doesn't ignore me. "You do? If you could fix the book-return slot, maybe you can also find my earring. What's your idea, Jelly?"

I point to a large plastic vacuum cleaner outside the shed. It has a small engine and a long hose. The lifeguards use it to suck debris out of the pool.

"That won't work," the lifeguard says. "The debris the vacuum cleaner sucks out of the pool goes right to the septic system."

"It doesn't have to," I say.

The lifeguard crosses his arms over his chest. "Of course it has to. That's how a pool vacuum works. I hate to say it, but I really don't think we'll find that earring."

Eloise's mother sniffles.

"That's how a pool vacuum *usually* works," I tell the lifeguard. "We could intercept the debris *before* it reaches the septic system. But we'll need..." I look around at the kids lying on towels, the other lifeguard on the lifeguard chair and groups of people clustered at picnic tables, having lunch or playing cards.

I raise my finger in the air.

Some of the people playing cards are elderly. What I need is a pair of nylons. It would be easy to find someone wearing them on a cool day. But I happen to know that some elderly women like to wear nylons even on hot summer days. I think I've heard it helps with their blood circulation.

"Wait here!" I tell the others. I head for a picnic table where a group of seniors is playing gin rummy. Sure enough, one of the women there is wearing nylon socks. "Er," I say, "excuse me. This is an unusual request."

The woman and her friends look surprised to see me.

"My friend's mom lost her earring in the pool. If I had a nylon sock, I could attach it to the vacuum and find the missing earring. Ma'am," I say, speaking directly to the woman wearing the nylons, "I know it's a lot to ask, but could I have one of your socks?"

"Would I get it back afterward?" the woman asks.

"Uh, not exactly. I think it might get stretched out, and the chlorine might not be good for it. But I'm sure Eloise's mother would get you another sock. Probably a pair since you can't buy just one."

When the old woman smiles I know she is going to say yes. "It is an unusual request," she says, reaching under the picnic table so she can pull off her sock. "But why not?"

It doesn't take me long to attach the sock to the hose. The woman who gave me her sock also gives me an elastic from her purse. I use it to secure the sock.

The lifeguard uses the refurbished equipment to vacuum the pool floor.

When he is finished, we gather around to see what debris has been collected inside the sock. The seniors who were playing gin rummy come to see too.

The lifeguard dumps the contents on a table.

Because it was my idea, I get to sort through the debris.

At first all I see are leaves. They are so wet they have turned black. There's a snail, and dice from a board game.

"How did dice get into the pool?" someone asks.

No one bothers answering. Because at exactly that moment, we see a gold shimmer, and something green catches the light.

It's the missing earring!

Chapter Six

Two days later it's pouring. It's still hot, but the sky is dark and the rain is coming down in sheets. The pool is closed on account of bad weather.

Joon and I play in the water anyhow.

We put on our bathing suits and run barefoot in Joon's front garden.

"You must be sorry you can't interview people today for your story about trouble in the lap lanes," Joon says.

"It's good to get a break when you do research," I tell Joon. "Miss Marston says researching a story can get very intense."

Someone walks by under a white umbrella with red polka dots. It's Eloise! She stops to chat. "It's a perfect day for going to the library," she says. "I'm on my way."

"It's a perfect day for playing in the rain," Joon says. "Why don't you get your bathing suit and join us?"

"I would—except I promised Ms. MacLean I'd help make posters. She wants to draw a crowd for the lecture series starting at the library later this week," Eloise says. "Why don't you two come to the library later?"

Joon's mother makes us chap chae for lunch. Chap chae is stir-fried sweet-potato

noodles with vegetables. Joon is better at using chopsticks than I am. We eat on the porch so we can watch the rain.

After lunch we head to the library. Joon and I want to borrow a DVD to watch later. But we can't agree on the kind of movie we want to see. I want a comedy. Joon wants a horror movie. "Maybe," I suggest, "we can manage to find something in between."

We're not the only kids who want to watch a movie today. Lots of kids are milling around, talking about movies they have seen and movies that are supposed to be good.

When one of the assistant librarians comes over, I think it's because she wants us to whisper. At the old library we weren't allowed to raise our voices.

Somehow everything about this library feels different. The assistant librarian just wants to know if there are other movies we want the library to order.

Because there are so many kids looking for movies, Joon and I go downstairs to visit the rare-books room.

The room smells like old paper. There are several glass cases with books inside. I spot an old copy of *Alice's Adventures in Wonderland*, opened to the first page. "Look," I say to Joon, "it's signed by the author!"

"That book must be worth a fortune," Joon says. "No wonder the library keeps it under glass."

We hear someone in the hallway just outside the room. It's Eloise. She has a pile of posters hanging over one arm.

"Jelly and Joon!" she says when she sees us. "I'm glad you came. There's something we need to talk about, Jelly."

"Do you want to talk to Jelly about how she saved the day and found your mother's missing earring?" Joon asks.

"No, it isn't that," Eloise says. The way she is looking at me makes me think something is wrong.

Eloise puts her posters down on one of the display cases. "Is it true, Jelly, that you've won many awards for your newspaper stories?"

"I don't like to boast," I say, "but yes, I have won a few awards."

"You have?" Joon says. "You've never mentioned that before."

"I don't like to boast," I say again.

"What kinds of awards have you won?" Joon asks.

"I won the…"—I have to think quickly—"the award for most promising young journalist in Canada. And also an award for investigative reporting."

"That's amazing," Joon says. "I'm so proud to be your friend, Jelly."

"Investigative reporting?" Eloise is watching my face in a way that makes me nervous. "I heard that Angelica Ledoux won a national newspaper award for writing feature stories."

"Feature stories," I say. "I don't know why I said investigative reporting. I meant feature stories."

"What did it feel like to win such an important award?" Joon asks.

"It was amazing," I tell her. The story is bubbling in my head the way soup or spaghetti sauce bubbles on the stove. "There was a prize banquet in Toronto.

I went there by train. First-class, of course. I had three strawberry milkshakes."

"Did you get motion sickness?" Joon asks.

"Not at all," I tell her.

Eloise shakes her head. "I smell something suspicious."

"All I smell is old paper," I say.

Eloise picks up one of the posters and unrolls it. "You know the lecture series I mentioned? Well, the first speaker is coming the day after tomorrow. She's a prize-winning journalist from the *Gazette*, and her name is Angelica Ledoux. And look," she says, pointing to a face on the poster. "This Angelica Ledoux doesn't look anything like you."

Joon spins around to look at me. Her eyes have a fiery look. "Jelly! Don't tell me you're making up stories again!"

Chapter Seven

Eloise has forgotten all about hanging up her posters. "Are you saying this isn't the first time Jelly has lied about who she is?" she asks Joon.

"That's exactly what I'm saying. When I first met Jelly at summer camp, she told us she was a princess. She had us make her bed and do her chores," Joon tells Eloise. "Then, when we were at the animal-rescue center, she made a boy named Leo believe she was a part-time lion trainer."

I don't like the way Eloise and Joon are talking to each other. It's as if they're best friends and I'm just some stranger.

"Excuse me," I say to Joon, "you left out the part of the story where I fixed the kayak when the rudder broke on our overnight camping trip. And also the part of the story where I rescued Mwezi the lioness when she escaped from her enclosure."

Joon and Eloise are so busy talking, they don't pay any attention to me.

"It isn't right to tell lies. Why do you think she does it?" Eloise asks Joon.

"My mother thinks she has an overactive imagination," Joon says. "My father thinks she needs more excitement in her life."

I don't like Joon and Eloise calling me *she*. I also don't like Joon's parents having opinions about me. And I don't like my friends talking about me as if I'm not even there!

"Uh, excuse me," I say, "but my name is Jelly. Not *she*. Look, I'm really sorry about pretending to be Angelica Ledoux."

Joon and Eloise don't even look at me. That's when I realize what they are doing—ignoring me. They're punishing me for lying!

I hate being ignored. So I tap Eloise's shoulder. She doesn't turn around. I tap again. "If you want to know why I make up stories, you should ask me, not Joon. I make them up because I—"

"La la la la la," Eloise starts to sing.

"Tra la la la la," Joon joins in.

They are trying to drown out the
sound of my voice.

Thinking the words *drown out*
reminds me of the pool. I tap Eloise's
shoulder again. "Did you forget how I
figured out a way to find your mother's
earring?" I ask her. "Doesn't that count
for anything?"

Eloise finally turns to face me. "I did
not forget how you figured out a way to

find my mother's earring. But I'm still upset that you lied to me."

"I said I was sorry. Do you think you could get over it?" I ask.

"Maybe. But not yet," Eloise says.

"Me too," Joon adds.

The two girls go back to ignoring me. They seem to have lots to talk about—movies, the pool, teachers they like, even Korean food. "Have you ever had chap chae?" Joon asks Eloise. "My mother makes it. Maybe you can come to my house sometime and try it."

"What about me? Can I come too?"

No answer.

"What am I supposed to do while you two ignore me and make plans to eat chap chae together?" I ask. I don't mean to shout, but the question comes out louder than I mean it to.

I don't expect an answer. So I'm surprised when Joon turns to me and says, "Why don't you work on your story, Jelly, since you're a prize-winning reporter?"

Joon is being sarcastic—teasing me for having told Eloise I was a prize-winning reporter. But working on my story isn't a bad idea. Besides, if Joon and Eloise aren't talking to me, it isn't like I have anything better to do.

There's an old-fashioned desk with an old-fashioned chair in the corner of the rare-books room. I sit down at the desk and take out all my notes. In all, I have interviewed five people, including the lifeguard and Eloise's mother.

I remember how Miss Marston said that before reporters start to write their stories, they review all their notes— and they look for a *hook*. The hook comes at the beginning of the story. It's called a hook because it's meant to hook readers so that they will read to the end.

Rereading my notes helps me forget that Joon and Eloise are ignoring me. I could use the lost earring for a hook. Or I could use the lifeguard saying there are fights every day in the lap lanes. Yes, that's a better hook than the lost earring. I'll keep the lost-earring incident for later. That way there will be a hopeful ending. Trouble grabs readers' interest, but no one wants to read about it nonstop.

I am starting to see the shape of my story—the beginning, middle and end.

Outside, the rain comes down even harder. I can hear it pelting against the windows.

I'm a little nervous about this story. What if I make spelling or grammatical mistakes? Even worse, what if it's boring?

But it's raining too hard to head home, so now is as good a time as any to begin my story about trouble in the lap lanes. If I make spelling or grammatical mistakes, I can fix them. If the story is boring, I can fix that too.

I start to write.

I write one sentence and then, because I don't like it, I cross it out. Being a reporter is harder than I thought.

The door to the rare-books room opens. It's Ms. MacLean. I recognize the woman with her—because her photo is on Eloise's posters.

It's Angelica Ledoux.

The real one.

And she has a dog.

Chapter Eight

"Hello, girls," Ms. MacLean says when she sees us. "I'd like you to meet—"

"Angelica Ledoux," the three of us say at the same time.

The dog—an apricot-colored pug with a wrinkly face—pulls on her leash and goes to sniff under one of the glass cases.

"Plug!" Angelica Ledoux says. "Come back here!" But the pug wags her tail and continues sniffing.

"What a cute dog!" Joon says. "But why'd you call her Plug?"

"Because it rhymes with *pug*," Angelica Ledoux explains. "And because it seemed to suit her."

"If you don't mind my asking, what are you doing here today?" Eloise asks her. "Your talk isn't until Friday. And why did you bring Plug?"

"I was nearby and thought I'd have a look at the library so I'd know what to expect." Angelica Ledoux is tall and has black hair and bangs that nearly cover her eyes. She has a serious voice. "I didn't want to leave Plug in the car. She hates storms."

"Did you bring a pen?" I ask her.

Angelica taps the outside of her purse. "In here," she says. "I never go anywhere without a pen—and a notebook.

Though many of the younger reporters take notes on their phones."

"I like pen and paper too," I say.

Eloise shoots me an annoyed look. Then she looks back at Angelica Ledoux. "That's Jelly," she says. "She's been pretending to be you."

I really wish she hadn't said that.

"Pretending to be me?" Angelica sounds more curious than angry. "Whatever for?"

"Jelly likes pretending to be other people. She once pretended to be a princess. And another time she pretended to be a lion trainer," Joon explains.

"How interesting," Angelica says, and for a minute I think she's going to whip out her pen and paper and start interviewing me.

Ms. MacLean puts her hands on her hips. "Do you mean to say Jelly was assuming Angelica Ledoux's identity?" she asks. "That's very wrong. People can get sent to jail for that sort of thing. The authorities call it *identity theft*."

I'm imagining myself in a prison cell, wearing a jumpsuit and living on bread and water. "I already apologized to Eloise," I say. "But I guess I need to apologize to you too." Though it's hard, I look into Angelica Ledoux's eyes. "I shouldn't have pretended to be you. It's just that...I really wish I could be a reporter. And when Eloise asked me whether I was the one who wrote the article about how people get good ideas, I couldn't resist saying it was me. It was an excellent article, by the way."

"Jelly is really good at making stuff up, and she's also good at repairing things," Joon chimes in. Something about the way she says it makes me think it won't be long till we are back on speaking terms.

"That's true. Jelly repaired the book-return slot," Ms. MacLean tells Angelica. "She used coconut oil."

Angelica grins. "How ingenious. Jelly, I'm going to forgive you for pretending to be me. It doesn't seem as if any real harm was done. But if you don't mind, I'd like to give you some advice. Reporters always tell the truth. If you really want to make things up, you should consider writing storybooks instead."

"I know it's wrong to tell lies. And like I said, I'm really sorry I pretended to be someone I'm not. I promise to try to be a better person. Then maybe one day I could be a reporter who writes storybooks on the side. Or a storybook writer who does reporting on the weekends."

Angelica taps her chin. "Maybe you could," she says. "As long as you don't get the two mixed up."

A boom of thunder interrupts our conversation. Angelica kneels down to pet Plug when the dog starts to whimper. "Don't worry, Plug," she says. "You're safe in here."

Water is still pelting down against the windows. Now a single bolt of silver lightning illuminates the gray sky.

Plug whimpers more loudly.

"Lightning freaks her out," Angelica says.

"You know what freaks me out?" Ms. MacLean asks, pointing to a wet spot on the floor. "A flood in the rare-books room!"

Chapter Nine

"Thank goodness the rare books are safe inside the glass cases," Joon says.

When Ms. MacLean looks up at the ceiling, we all look up too. There's no sign of moisture. The leak isn't up there. Then Ms. MacLean looks down at the pool of water on the floor. She bites her lip. "The rare books are safe for now. But see how the pool of water

is growing?" Sure enough, the pool is twice the size it was before. "Even if the water doesn't rise as high as the glass cases, too much moisture in this room can endanger our book collection. I need to call the contractor who managed the construction of this library!"

The thunder gets louder and the lightning more frequent. Poor Plug is starting to pant.

Angelica Ledoux may be a prize-winning reporter, but she isn't very good at comforting pets.

Ms. MacLean is on her cell phone, shouting at the contractor. "I know you're busy with important new projects, but this is a brand-new library, and there shouldn't be a flood in our rare-books room. That's right—a flood! You need to drop whatever you're doing and get over here! No! This can't wait until tomorrow!"

Eloise taps me on the shoulder.

"Aren't you supposed to be angry with me?" I ask her.

"This isn't a good time to discuss that," she says. "I was wondering...since you're so good at repairs, could you find a way to stop the flood?"

Joon taps my other shoulder. "Jelly, I was wondering...since you're so good with lions, do you think there's something you could do to calm that dog down?"

It's impossible for one person to solve two problems at once. I need to make a decision. Ms. MacLean is telephoning a plumber. Maybe they will be able to come straightaway. As for Plug, she is running around in circles, whimpering, snorting, panting and bumping into the glass bookcases.

"Plug!" Angelica shouts. "You're making a bad situation worse."

"I don't think dogs understand English," Eloise tells her.

"Shouting at Plug will only make her more anxious," I add.

"Well then, what am I supposed I do?" Now Angelica is shouting at *me*. Which doesn't seem fair.

I could try chasing Plug around the room. Tiring her out might help calm her down. But chasing Plug could also make her more agitated.

So I decide to try something else. I kneel down on the floor and say, "Plug," in my most soothing voice. But another boom of thunder drowns out my voice.

Plug is shaking like a kid getting out of the pool on a cold day.

"Plug," I say again. This time Plug looks at me. And when I say "Plug" a third time, she stops in her tracks.

I can tell from Plug's eyes and the way she is shaking that she is still afraid. "Plug," I say, "did I tell you about the story I'm writing on trouble in the lap lanes?"

"Trouble in the lap lanes?" Angelica Ledoux says. "How interesting."

"Shhh," Joon says to Angelica. "Don't interrupt Jelly. She's found a way to get Plug to sit still!"

Sure enough, Plug is resting on her haunches, her eyes glued to my face.

"There were two swimmers having a terrible argument. One was doing the dog paddle," I continue.

Plug wags her curly tail. I knew she'd like the part about the dog paddle.

"You might know that the dog paddle is kind of a slow stroke. So the swimmer behind the person doing the dog paddle got annoyed. 'The lap lane is no place for the dog paddle!' the second swimmer yelled."

I meet Plug's gaze. "Guess what the swimmer who was doing the dog paddle did next?" I'm stalling for time because

I haven't exactly figured out the rest of my story.

Plug barks.

"Exactly!" I say. "The swimmer doing the dog paddle started to bark. Some kids were watching the argument from the shallow end. One boy started to meow like a cat. A girl mooed like a cow. And another kid chirped like a bird. And then you know what happened?"

"What?" Eloise asks. Which is how I know she is enjoying my story too.

"Everyone started to laugh. Even the two swimmers who were fighting."

Eloise, Joon and Angelica Ledoux clap.

"I'm not finished with my story," I tell them. "I left the best part for last. Just as everyone was making animal noises and laughing, an apricot-colored pug named Plug"—Plug wags her tail when I mention her—"jumped into the lap lane and started doing the dog paddle. And you know what? She was faster than all the other swimmers!"

Plug is listening so intently that she doesn't even notice when there is another boom of thunder and two more flashes of lightning.

Ms. MacLean puts her cell phone back into her pocket. "The plumber is busy until the day after tomorrow. Jelly, you did a good job of distracting Plug with your story. Now, if you don't mind, could you try to do something about this flood?"

Chapter Ten

"It looks like that dog is your new best friend," Joon says.

Since I told Plug the story about the lap lane, she's been following me around like a dog (which makes sense since she is one).

"Everyone needs a best friend," I tell Joon.

"*I'm* your best friend," Joon says.

"Really? Even if I made up another story and pretended to be someone I wasn't?"

"Even if," Joon says.

When I squeeze Joon's hand, Plug snorts.

The puddle in the rare-books room is getting bigger.

I watch the water spreading. It seems to be coming from behind a wall. "I think the leak is in the next room," I say.

Ms. MacLean wipes her forehead. "That's the boiler room," she says.

When she opens the door to that room, we see an even larger puddle on the floor. "Is there a drain in here?" I ask Ms. MacLean.

"It's just behind the furnace."

I squat down and feel the metal grates of a drain. Water is trickling out of it. "I think we've found the problem," I say.

Ms. MacLean wrings her hands. "If only the contractor could get over here—or we could find a plumber."

"What about the custodian?" Eloise says. "Don't tell me it's his day off again."

Ms. MacLean sighs. "It's his day off again," she says.

"We don't need a custodian or a contractor or a plumber," Joon tells Ms. MacLean. "We have Jelly!"

"I've fixed a leaky roof, repaired a kayak, built a wheelchair ramp, found an escaped lioness, fixed a book-return slot, found a missing earring and calmed down a nervous pug, but I've never done any plumbing repairs," I say.

"You've done all those things?" asks Angelica Ledoux.

"It's probably a broken water main," I say. "The city will fix that. In the meantime, we have to find a way to stop the water from coming up from this drain." I'm talking to myself, which sometimes happens when I am solving a problem.

"Joon, can you grab the towel from my backpack?"

Jewel comes back with my towel and hers too. I fold the towels in two and lay them over the drain. We hear a *glug glug* as the flow of water comes to a stop.

"What a great idea!" Eloise says.

"Not so great, actually," I say. "Once the towels are soaked, they won't be much of a barrier. They're just a temporary measure while I try to come up with a better solution."

Plug snorts.

"I think Plug wants another story," Joon says.

But right now I'm not thinking about stories.

I'm thinking about how to stop this flood.

Plug.

Why didn't I think of it before?

"Come here, Plug," I say, tapping my knee. Plug runs to me, then scurries away again.

"She wants you to chase her," Eloise says.

"I can't play now," I tell Plug.

Plug is on her haunches, looking at me from across the boiler room.

"Come here, Plug," I coax.

Plug won't budge.

"Those towels are getting soaked," Angelica Ledoux says.

I can't do this without Plug. I squat down lower and look into Plug's eyes. "Wanna hear the rest of the story?"

Plug comes back over. "If you could sit right here," I tell her, pointing to the drain. Plug's bottom is just the right size to seal the drain.

"It's only a temporary solution," I tell Ms. MacLean, "but it should do until you find a better plug or the city shuts off the water."

"That pug really is a plug," Joon says, and everyone laughs.

At first Plug is a little startled by the water underneath her. But once I get back into my story, she settles down.

"This pug named Plug was so amazing at the dog paddle that she ended up competing in the Doggie Olympics," I say.

Eloise sighs loudly. "There's no such thing as Doggie Olympics."

Joon shushes Eloise.

"Plug didn't win gold the first year. She won bronze. But four years later, she won gold. Plug made headlines around the world. And guess who got to write the story about her for the *Gazette*? Me! Angelica, junior reporter! When Plug's owner, Angelica Ledoux, went on holidays, guess who dog-sat for Plug?"

"Angelica, junior reporter!" Joon calls out.

Plug snorts and wags her curly tail without moving from her spot over the drain.

Chapter Eleven

The boiler room is getting crowded.

The first one to turn up is a city official. "There's a broken water main under the street," he announces.

"Jelly figured that out already," Ms. MacLean tells him.

"We'll be shutting down the water any minute now," the city official says. "What's that dog doing over there?"

"That's Plug. She helped Jelly stop the rare-books room from flooding," Angelica Ledoux explains.

The next one to turn up is Monsieur St-Onge, the *Gazette* photographer. He seems surprised to find Angelica Ledoux in the boiler room. She explains about wanting to visit the library before her talk. She also tells him how I stopped the flood—with Plug's help.

Monsieur St-Onge wants to take a photograph of Plug sitting on the drain, with me petting her.

Then the custodian turns up.

"What are you doing here? It's your day off," Ms. MacLean says.

"When I heard that rain coming down, I thought I'd pop over to check on things. You know how new buildings can be," he explains. "Also, my wife made a banana bread this morning, and I brought some for everyone."

"Banana bread is my favorite!" Joon calls out.

The custodian mops up the water.

Even Plug gets a chunk of banana bread.

"I think Plug has the perfect personality for our upcoming Bow Wow reading program," Ms. MacLean tells Angelica Ledoux. "She can listen to children read or tell stories. Could you bring her to the library on Tuesdays at four o'clock sharp?"

Angelica Ledoux shakes her head. "I have to be in the newsroom at that hour." She looks at me. "Jelly, could you pick Plug up and bring her here for the Bow Wow program? I'd pay you, of course."

"Minimum wage?" Joon asks.

"That sounds like a great job," I tell Angelica Ledoux.

"In addition to paying minimum wage, I'm going to offer you another treat," Angelica says.

Plug jumps up from her spot on the drain when she hears the word *treat*. Luckily, the city has turned off the water.

"It's not a treat for you, Plug," Angelica says. "It's for Jelly. Plug wasn't the only one who enjoyed your stories, Jelly. I did too. I want to help you develop your writing. I want to be your mentor."

"Are you going to help Jelly with her newspaper writing or with the stories she invents?" Eloise asks.

"Newspaper stories are my specialty. I don't think Jelly needs much help making up stories."

"Thank you so much," I say. "That sounds amazing."

I turn to Joon and Eloise. "So how do you two feel now about calling me Jelly, junior reporter?"

Excerpt from the first book in the series,

Princess ANGELICA
Camp Catastrophe

"Did I ever tell you we have an elevator?" I ask Maddie.

Her brown eyes widen. "You never mentioned it. But that is seriously cool. Where is it?"

Maddie believes all my stories. It's one of the reasons she's my best friend.

Another reason is that she is super kind. It also helps that Maddie lives two doors down, which is handy, especially during snowstorms.

"Our elevator is at the back of my parents' closet."

"Where does it go to?"

Maddie always asks a lot of questions. Luckily, I am great at coming up with answers.

"To the attic."

"Can we ride it?"

I was hoping she would ask. "Yup. There's just one hitch." I pause. That will make her even more eager for a ride on our elevator. "I have to blindfold you." I make it sound like blindfolding your best friend is no big deal.

"Blindfold me? Jelly, is this one of your stories?"

I make a huffing sound so she will know I am insulted. "Of *course* not.

The blindfold is for insurance purposes. So you won't sue." My parents are both lawyers, so I know a lot about suing.

When we get to my parents' bedroom, I grab a dark scarf from my mother's drawer and tie it over Maddie's eyes.

"Can you see anything?"

"Not a thing."

"Perfect."

I spin her around three times. Then I lead her into my parents' closet. I guide her so she doesn't trip over the shoes and boots. "Okay," I tell her. "We're inside the elevator now."

I clang together two wire hangers and stamp my feet on the closet floor. "Whoa," I say. "We're going up. I feel it in my stomach."

"Me too," says Maddie.

I grin. My plan is working.

"What's up in your attic?" she asks.

"Skeletons." It's the first thing that pops into my head.

"Cool."

"We're nearly there," I tell her. I clang together the wire hangers again. "The elevator doors are about to open."

"I can't believe I have a friend who has her own elevator," Maddie says to herself.

"We're there." I grab her elbow and lead her out of the closet. "Are you ready to see skeletons? Do you promise you won't sue?"

"Yes and yes." Maddie's voice catches in her throat. That is probably because she has never seen a skeleton before.

I spin Maddie around three more times—and untie the scarf. "Ta-dum!"

Maddie is trembling.

Because the lights are out in my parents' bedroom, it takes her a minute to realize what's going on.

There are no skeletons.

We are not in the attic.

There is no elevator.

Maddie hops up and down. "Jelly," she cries out, "you made that story up!"

There is another reason why Maddie is my best friend.

Other kids might get angry.

Not Maddie.

Because a second later the two of us are laughing so hard we end up rolling around on the floor in my parents' bedroom.

MONIQUE POLAK has written many novels for young adults, including her historical novel *What World is Left*, which won the 2009 Quebec Writers' Federation Prize for Children's and Young Adult Literature. When not writing award-winning books, Monique teaches English and humanities at Marianopolis College in Montreal. She is also an active freelance journalist.